SAM
THE GARBAGE HOUND

BY CHARNAN SIMON

ILLUSTRATED BY GARY BIALKE

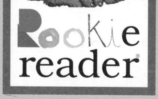

Rookie reader®

SCHOLASTIC INC.

New York   Toronto   London   Auckland   Sydney
Mexico City   New Delhi   Hong Kong   Buenos Aires

For the real Sam and all his friends:
Emma, Dasher, Sadie, Mocha, Addie, Rocky, Belle, Sophie, Annie, Lungi,
Gretchen, Bear, Scout, Cooper, Toby, Dusty, Mollie, Cookie, Rags, Josh, Pal,
and the rest of the dogs in the woods

— C. S.

To Auggie, Wiley, and Barkley

— G. B.

ISBN 0-516-24143-5

12 11 10 9 8 7   4 5 6 7/0

Printed in the U.S.A.   10

First Scholastic club printing, May 2002

Sam was a garbage hound.

JUNK

CAUTION:
DO NOT
PLAY ON
OR AROUND

He lived at the dump.

He ate canned food.

6

8

He slept in a snug bed.

He chased flies for fun.

It was a good life,

but Sam was lonely.

One day Rosie and her mother
came to the dump.

When they left,
Sam went with them.

19

Now Sam lives in a house.

He still eats canned food.

He still sleeps in a snug bed.

25

And he still chases flies for fun.

26

Sam is not lonely anymore.

But he will always be
a garbage hound.

Word List (53 Words)

a	came	for	is	now	them
always	canned	fun	it	one	they
and	chased	garbage	left	Rosie	to
anymore	chases	good	life	Sam	was
at	day	he	lived	sleeps	went
ate	dump	her	lives	slept	when
be	eats	hound	lonely	snug	will
bed	flies	house	mother	still	with
but	food	in	not	the	

About the Author

Charnan Simon lives in Madison, Wisconsin, with her husband, Tom Kazunas, her daughters, Ariel and Hana, and the real Sam, who is part collie and part golden retriever. This Sam makes up for his lack of taste and manners by his sunny disposition, affectionate nature, and boundless energy.

Charnan used to be an editor at *Cricket* magazine and sometimes works at a children's bookstore called Pooh Corner. She spends much of her time reading and writing books, enjoying her family, and buying shoes to replace the ones Sam eats for breakfast!

About the Illustrator

Born in the midwest and trained as an illustrator while still a pup, Gary Bialke journeyed to the soggy environs of the Pacific Northwest to pursu an animation career. After ten years of creative bliss in this field, his job was replaced by a computer.

Gary now resides in Portland, Oregon, with three large dogs and vacuum cleaner. He hopes to one day find enough success as an artist t give up his paper route.